Matthew 6:34
—J.D.

To B.S.
Thank you for encouraging me every day!
Love always
—K.D.

Pete the Cat: Crayons Rock!
Text copyright © 2020 by Kimberly and James Dean
Illustrations copyright © 2020 by James Dean
Pete the Cat is a registered trademark of Pete the Cat, LLC.
All rights reserved. Printed in Italy.
No part of this book may be used or reproduced in any manner whatsoever without
written permission except in the case of brief quotations embodied in critical articles and reviews.
For information address HarperCollins Children's Books, a division of HarperCollins Publishers,
195 Broadway, New York, NY 10007.
www.harpercollinschildrens.com
ISBN 978-0-06-286855-8
The artist used pen and ink with watercolor and acrylic paint on
300lb press paper to create the illustrations for this book.
21 22 23 24   RTLO   10 9 8 7 6 5 4 3 2
❖
First Edition

Kimberly & James Dean

Pete the Cat
Crayons Rock!

HARPER

An Imprint of HarperCollinsPublishers

KEY WEST

Pete loves his big box of groovy crayons!
He loves to draw things like cars, trucks,
flowers, and trees.
And most of all . . . the big blue sea.

From rockin' red
to cool cat blue,
with a box of crayons,
there's nothing
Pete can't do!

One day Pete decided to draw something new . . .

Using lots of colors is so much fun.
Pete wanted to use every one.
He scribbled and drew a great big
smile. His drawings were groovy
and rockin' with style!

Pete was proud of the pictures he drew.
He hoped his friends would dig them, too.

Pete showed Grumpy Toad first.

Grumpy Toad said, "This doesn't look right. Those colors are way too bright."

Pete thought,

"HEY, NO SWEAT. THAT'S ALL RIGHT!"

Pete showed Gus his picture, too.

Gus asked, "Who is this supposed to be? It doesn't really look like me."

Pete thought,

"HEY, NO SWEAT. THAT'S ALL RIGHT!"

Pete finally showed Callie her picture.

Callie said, "This one is fine, but it feels like something's missing from mine."

Pete said,

"WHAT A

MESS!"

"Bummer. I guess my drawings aren't the best."
Pete started to frown. He put his crayons down.

In art class the teacher asked, "Pete what are you going to make?"
"I don't know—I'm afraid of making a mistake!"

Pete looked around.

Gus drew the coooooolest superheroes.

Callie's flowers were awesome! Out-of-sight!

Grumpy's motorcycle was just right!

Pete's heart sank. His paper was blank.

The gang looked at Pete and said,
"No sweat! It's all right!
"It doesn't have to be just right.

"Your art is cool because it's YOU.
Your art is so unique.

"Grab your groovy box of crayons.
Show us your technique!"

The teacher agreed. "Art should be fun!
Art is for everyone!

"From rockin' red
to cool cat blue,
with a box of crayons,
there's nothing you can't do!"

Pete smiled. "There are no rules. It's no big deal! Art is about how it makes you feel!"

Pete loved his cool art.
That's the one thing Pete knew.
Suddenly, Pete knew exactly what to do.

He tried again!

Instead of drawing them one by one,

Pete drew the whole gang, just having fun!

Grumpy Toad, Gus, and Callie agreed
Pete's picture was off the charts!
See? That's the groovy thing about art.